Pancakes soft and piping hot
With butter rolling off the top,
Dripping with honey,
All golden and runny,
Yummy!

BUT at home the ingredients are often lacking.
It's enough to send poor Polly packing!

"The eggs have all been used up.
There's not enough milk to fill a cup.
It's certainly not a laughing matter
That there's not even flour to make the batter!"

"OH WHAT DOES IT TAKE
TO GET A PANCAKE?"

Mum **moans** and **groans**,

"I certainly have enough to do.

Polly, **oh Polly**,

it's not all about **you!**"

"There are many floors to be swept
And dishes to soak!
There's no time left
To even iron my coat!"

"The sofa smells musty,
And everything's dusty!
Just how can I think of flour, milk and eggs
When there's not even time to wax my legs?"

So Polly, fed up with things as they stand,
Decides she must take matters in hand.
What would certainly help indeed
Is to never, ever be in need
Of the ingredients it takes
To make piles of pancakes!

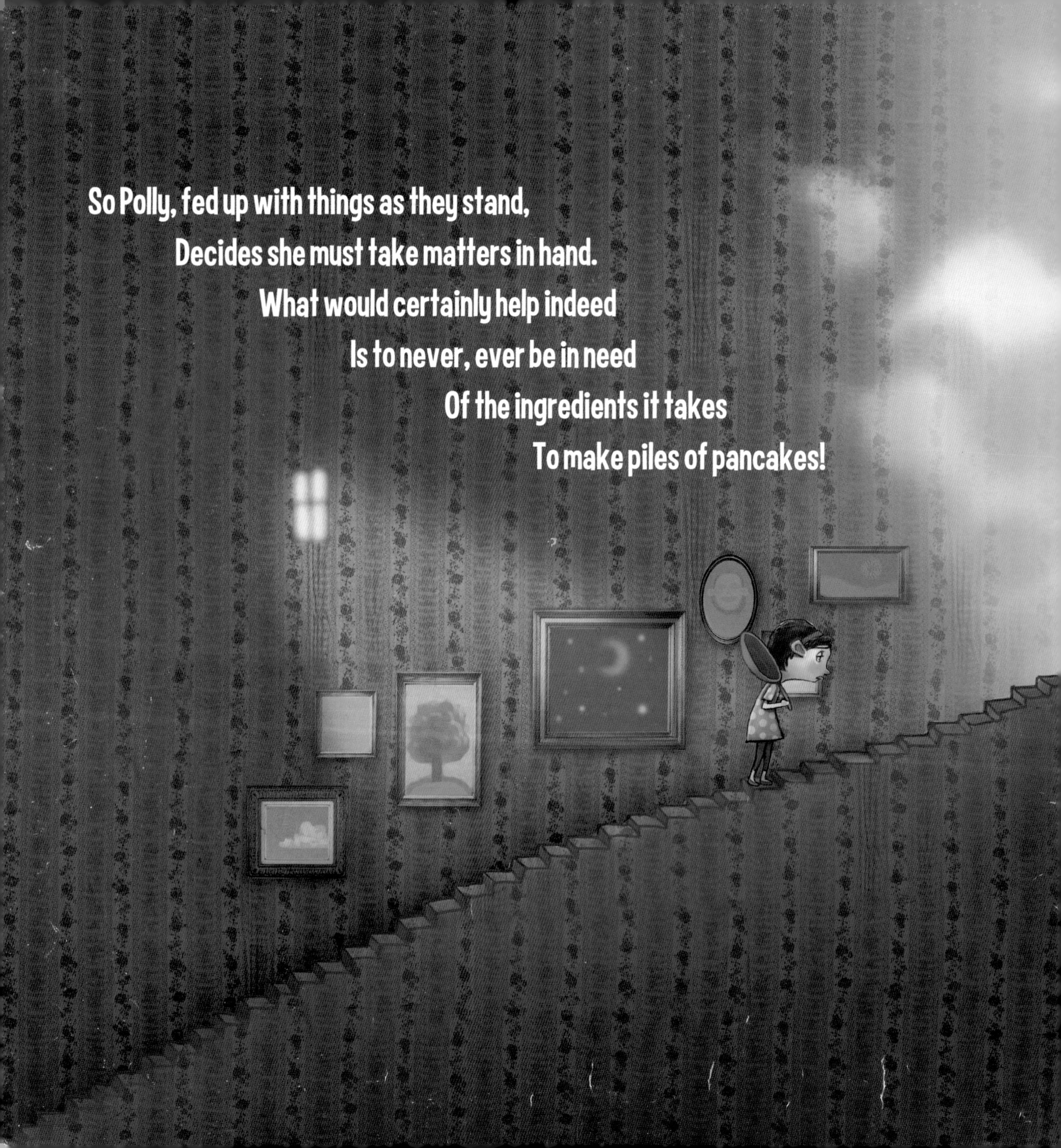

"If only I had a **humungous** mountain of flour
And a whole lot of eggs **piled** into a tower,
Enough milk to **fill** a lake...
So many pancakes I could make!"

So Polly's plan takes shape in her head.

A cow in the shed to give milk by the litre,

ens in the yard to lay eggs by the metre.

Bees to make honey

Shouldn't cost too much money.

Sacks of flour in a pile,

Oh, it makes Polly smile

To think with delight

Of the pancakes she'll eat

from **noon** until **night!**

Using mum's credit card
Surely can't be that hard.
How easy it is to just pick up the phone
And pay for these things
to be sent to her home!

The cow is so grand,
In the shed she'll stand.
The hens madly cackle and cluck
While sacks of flour arrive in a truck.

FLOUR
POWER

In the garden, a hive filled with buzzing bees
Warns intruders to stay away, please!
Bees like to be busy and left on their own
To fill with honey their sweet honeycomb.
HONEY

Everything is going according to plan.
Pretty soon we'll be ready to heat up the pan!

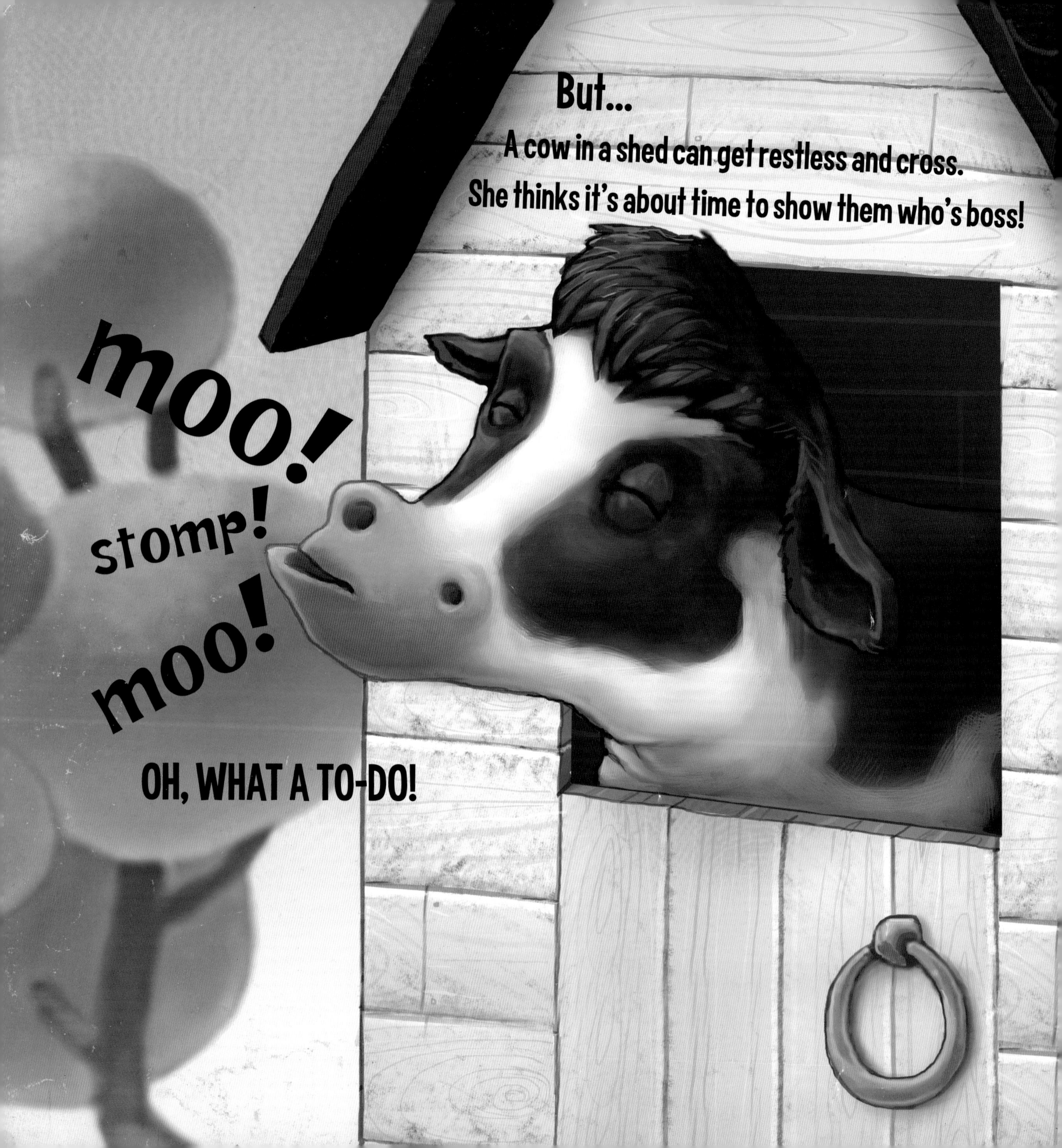
But...
A cow in a shed can get restless and cross.
She thinks it's about time to show them who's boss!
moo!
stomp!
moo!
OH, WHAT A TO-DO!

The noise is so loud
That it soon draws a crowd.
The neighbours all gather around
To ask, "Just what is that sound?"
mmmmooooooooo!

Now the hens, all frenzied and wild,
Waddle to where the sacks are piled.
There they begin to peck and pluck
And soon the yard is full of white muck!
The flour, the flour!
They'll spill it in an hour!
FLOUR
The neighbours are talking
And everyone's gawking...

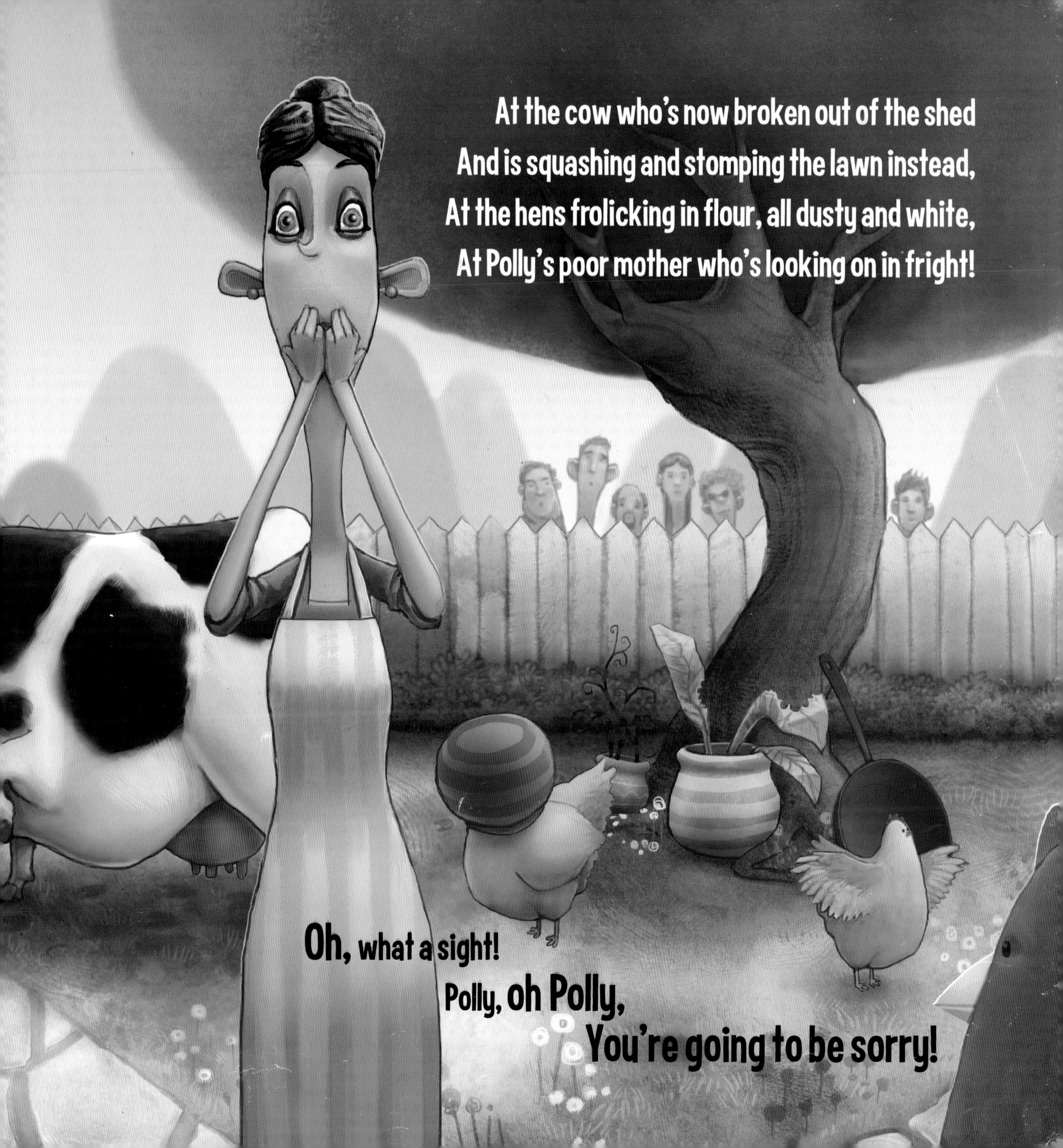

At the cow who's now broken out of the shed
And is squashing and stomping the lawn instead,
At the hens frolicking in flour, all dusty and white,
At Polly's poor mother who's looking on in fright!

Oh, what a sight!

Polly, oh Polly,
You're going to be sorry!

The cow has now totally **eaten** the lawn,

Leaving it all so short and **shorn.**

And the bushes have been completely **chomped**

While everything else is utterly **stomped!**

There are **dusty** hens all over the place

And a mask of **flour on everyone's face.**

The bee hive has been overturned on the lawn.
EEEEK! Here they all come in an angry swarm,
A thick, raging mass of stinging bees!

Why, *oh* why were they *not left* in peace?

“I am so very sorry...”

says poor Polly.

“How was I honestly to know
that this would turn
into such a show?”

Polly moans and shakes her head
Then looks around to find
That she's still in bed!

"Oh my goodness, gracious me!
How relieved can a girl be?

Fortunately for me
It would oh-so-luckily seem
That this whole mess was just a DREAM!"

"If I've been lying up here in bed
There can't be a cow breaking up the shed
Or a clutch of wild hens running madly around

Or a blanket of flour downstairs on the ground!
Oh, I'm glad that great mess was a dream and not real.
Still I feel like I've been through an awful ordeal!"

Later Mum asks Polly
what she would like with her tea.
"How about a pancake
my sweet honey pea?"
"Oh nooooo thanks Mum!
Certainly not for me!
Today I'm just not in the mood,
There's no way I could face my favourite food."

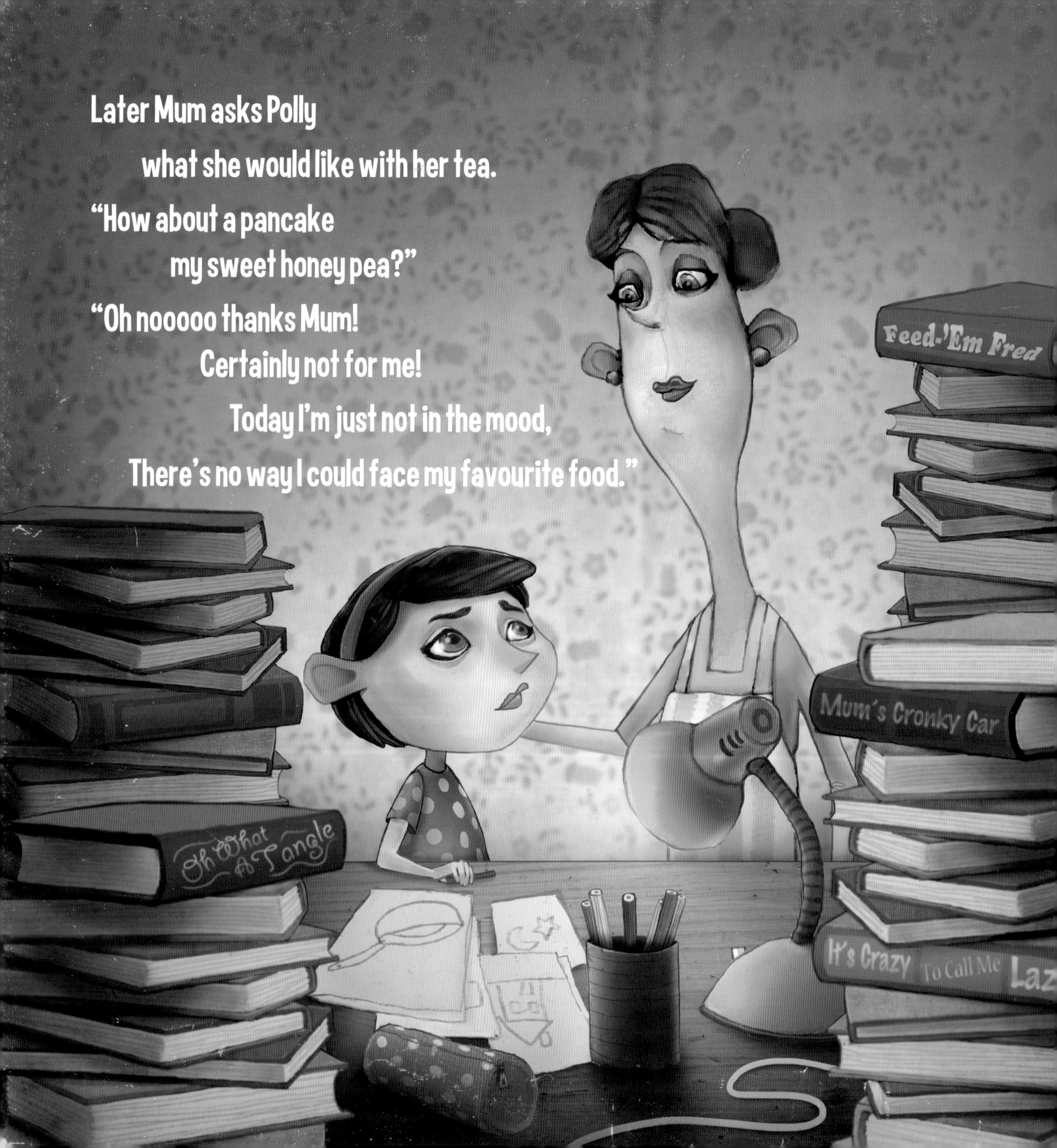

"Do you have something else like a fish-pie instead?
Something simple that won't make a mess in my head!"

The End

Polly's Easy-Peasy Pancakes

INGREDIENTS:

110g/4oz plain flour, sifted

Pinch of salt

2 eggs

200ml/7fl oz milk
mixed with 75ml/3fl oz water

50g/2oz butter

YOU'LL ALSO NEED:

A flat-bottomed frying pan, a sieve, a mixing bowl, a whisk or fork, a big spoon or ladle, a spatula, a bit of butter to grease your frying pan and a good appetite!

METHOD:

1. Using the sieve, sift the flour and salt into a large bowl.
2. Make a well (a big hole) in the centre of this mixture and break the eggs into it.
3. Then begin whisking the eggs with a whisk or fork until smooth.
4. Next gradually add small quantities of the milk and water mixture. Keep whisking!
5. Heat your frying pan over medium heat. Add a bit of butter and swish it around the pan to prevent the pancakes from sticking.
6. Now get the pan really hot, then turn the heat back down to medium. Pour a big spoonful of pancake batter into the pan and tip it around from side to side to get the base evenly coated.
7. Let your pancake cook until you see bubbles forming on the top.
8. Now you can turn the pancake over using a spatula so the other side can cook.
9. Leave the pancake on the pan for another minute.
10. Then lift the pancake off the pan with the spatula.
11. Do this again and again until you have a huge pile of pancakes...

TOPPING IDEAS:

Polly loves her pancakes piping hot, with butter and honey rolling off the top! You could also try topping them with sugar and lemon, chocolate and strawberries or banana and syrup! YUMMY!!

fun + games

Top This!

What's the topping going to be on the pancakes?

Find the Pans...

There are 14 frying pans in the pages of this story. See if you can spot them all.

For a little help go to www.anitapouroulis.com/pancakes

Find the following words in the word search below:

PANCAKE MILK
EGGS HONEY
FLOUR LEMON

T	P	P	P	M	I	L	K
O	K	A	E	W	I	A	S
L	H	O	N	E	Y	M	N
P	E	A	A	C	J	N	O
N	K	M	L	P	A	K	W
U	F	L	O	U	R	K	X
S	G	G	E	N	F	T	E

Pancake Pandemonium app

If you enjoyed reading this book then check out the interactive app version - available for the ipad, iphone and android devices.

SPECIAL FEATURES

- Touch and play - interact with the characters, make them jump into life!
- Narration and word-highlighting options.
- Hear the Pancake Pandemonium theme music and SFX throughout.
- Find the hidden items hidden in the app to unlock the bonus game!

THINGS TO TRY

- Hoover up the cat (don't worry she likes it)
- Help Polly's mum tidy up the kitchen.
- Send Polly into the dragon's lair to steal the pancakes!
- Play the bonus game!

Visit www.digitalleaf.co.uk for more stories and apps

facebook: digitalleafuk twitter: digitalleafuk